Chanukah on the Prairie

Burt E. Schuman

Illustrated by
Rosalind Charney Kaye

UAHC Press • *New York, New York*

For all the members, past and present,
of B'nai Israel Congregation
of Grand Forks, North Dakota,
whose congregation I had the honor
of serving as a student rabbi.
— BES

In loving memory of a
wonderful character—Uncle Lou.
— RCK

Text © 2003 by Burt E. Schuman
Illustrations © 2003 by Rosalind Charney Kaye
Manufactured in the United States of America
10 9 8 7 6 5 4 3 2 1

Author's Note

Jews began settling in Grand Forks, North Dakota, as early as 1881. Some came to establish homesteads on federal lands and others to establish businesses in this growing railroad community. By the 1890s, an influx of Eastern European Jewish immigrants had established a significant Jewish community with kosher shops, a synagogue, a cemetery, and a *mikveh* (ritual bath). Many of those immigrants were encouraged to settle in the region by representatives of the Jewish Agricultural Society and the Hebrew Immigrant Aid Society.

In 1891, Rabbi Benjamin Papermaster arrived from Lithuania and quickly organized a congregation. In 1893, B'nai Israel Synagogue erected its first building. Rabbi Papermaster served as spiritual leader of the congregation through the early 1930s. He died in 1934 and was succeeded by his son, Rabbi Isadore Papermaster. B'nai Israel Synagogue of Grand Forks still exists today, and is a member of the UAHC. I first became interested in the history of the congregation when I served as a student rabbi there during my time at Hebrew Union College-Jewish Institute of Religion.

It was a dry summer and a dry fall for the villagers of Nadworna, a little village in Eastern Galicia. The wheat crop had failed, and for Jew and non-Jew alike this meant hard times. Food was scarce in the town, and few of the farmers could afford to buy what the Jews had to offer.

"It will be a grim Rosh HaShanah," sighed Reb Yitzchak Zalcman, a silversmith and watchmaker.

"And a cold and hungry winter too," sighed his wife Frumeh.

Together, they let out a great big groan.

Neither Reb Yitzchak nor Frumeh had the heart to tell their children, eight-year-old Daniel and ten-year-old Miriam, that they were thinking of leaving Nadworna. They had been born in Nadworna, just like their parents and grandparents before them. The Zalcmans, like all the Jews of Nadworna, loved the Austrian Emperor, Franz Josef II, whom the Jews of Galicia lovingly called "Fraym Yossel." Under his rule, the Jews lived in safety and peace, though they were often very poor.

"But Fraym Yossel won't put bread on our table or shoes on our children's feet," grumbled Reb Mottel Eisenstein as he and Yitzchak sat next to each other in *shul*. "There is only one thing to do: leave Nadworna, leave Europe, and go to America!"

"America," thought Reb Yitzchak to himself, "*die Goldene Medineh*, the Golden Land, where a poor Jew from the shtetl could become a millionaire."

"America?" cried Frumeh. "What will we do in America? How will we survive?"

"America!" shouted Miriam.

"America," shouted Daniel, "where a Jew can truly be somebody!"

"Yes, *Tateh-Mameh*," they shouted. "Let's go to America!"

Three weeks later, the Zalcmans were busy packing for America. They sold everything they could, except for their Shabbat candlesticks and the little bit that they could carry with them. They made hurried farewells as their friends and neighbors came to see them off.

For three days and nights, the Zalcmans rode in a cramped train compartment. Plains turned into hills, and hills turned into mountains, again and again. Finally the train chugged past factories and warehouses and came to a noisy halt in the port of Hamburg, Germany.

The next morning they boarded the ship. For twelve days, the Zalcmans huddled together in steerage, their stomachs rising and falling with the rough waves of the North Atlantic. Finally someone shouted, *"Der breg fun America!"*—"The American coastline!"—and all the children on board rushed toward the railing.

Past the Verazzano Narrows, she came into focus, the lady of the harbor, the Statue of Liberty. Miriam and Daniel could not stop cheering and shouting.

They filed off the ship and took the ferry to Ellis Island, where they spent hours going to one line after another and being asked the same questions over and over. Just as they were about to board a ferry for New York, a frantic young man bounded up to them waving his arms and shouting, *"Yidn, Yidn!"*—"Jews, Jews!"

"Please don't take that ferry to New York. If you do, you'll end up living and working in terrible conditions! Those streets are not paved with gold, but with cinders, soot, sweat, and germs! We want to help you find a better future."

The young man offered the Zalcmans free train tickets to a place called Grand Forks, North Dakota. Reb Yitzchak and Frumeh looked at each other and made a quick decision. They had never before heard of such a place. But the chance to live the life of a farmer in the fresh air and open spaces of the prairie sounded better than city living.

The stranger tried to assure them that they were making the right choice. "Yes," he said, smiling. "There are Jews there, and kosher markets, and a *shul*. I'll wire the head of the Jewish community that you're coming. You'll be surprised to see how much it feels like home."

The family took the ferry west, to Hoboken, New Jersey, and soon were on a train for the Dakotas. The coastline blended into mountains, and mountains into forests . . .

. . . forests into rolling hills, and rolling hills into broad plains that reminded them of Eastern Galicia. Frumeh sighed with happiness at the familiar sights.

They had been on the train for nearly two whole days when at last they heard the conductor call out, "Grand Forks." The Zalcmans lumbered out of the train, carrying, lifting, pushing, and dragging their bags among them. Once they were on the platform, a man in a fur hat, fur-lined coat, and gray beard waved hurriedly in their direction.

"Shalom aleichem!" he shouted. "Welcome to Grand Forks!"

"Aleichem shalom!" Reb Yitzchak responded and hurried to shake the man's hand.

"My name is Shmuel Rabinovitch, and I am the president of the Jewish Community Council," he said in Yiddish. "Welcome to Grand Forks. Welcome to America!"

The Zalcmans looked around with a mixture of joy and puzzlement. Past the neat center of town with its white frame houses and its handsome red brick buildings lay a vast prairie, as vast as the eye could see and the mind could imagine. So different and yet so familiar. Though it was November, they could imagine the rustling of millions of sheaves of wheat.

Reb Rabinovitch had already arranged everything. A job for Reb Yitzchak in Mr. Slotkin's watch and clock repair shop, a furnished apartment on the top floor of Mrs. Shapiro's house on Sixth Street, English lessons with Mr. Bergson, who also taught in the High School. An icebox filled with kosher meat and produce, and cupboards filled with flour, sugar, canned fish and other staples—all put together by the Sisterhood of the local synagogue, Congregation B'nai Israel. Frumeh was stunned.

The children enrolled in school and soon realized that they were not the only ones who needed to learn English. There were children from Norway, Sweden and Finland. There were also Polish, Ukrainian, and German children, as well as Jews—just like in Galicia.

The women of the Sisterhood lovingly sewed and embroidered curtains for the ark and mantles for the Torah scrolls, and they invited Frumeh to join them. When they were finished, they made quilts and bedding for the spring, when the Zalcmans would be going out into the fields, to claim a plot of land for themselves and build a sod house to stake their claim.

Meanwhile the women shared stories of life in their new land, traded recipes and other useful information, and gossiped—just like in Galicia.

Miriam and David joined the other Jewish boys and girls for Hebrew lessons with Rabbi Benjamin Papermaster, the rabbi of Congregation B'nai Israel. This was different than in Galicia, where only boys studied Hebrew.

Rabbi Papermaster had a beautiful tenor voice, like the great cantors of Cracow and Lemberg. And he had a terrible temper as well—just like in Galicia.

Reb Yitzchak discovered that after morning prayer, B'nai Israel's officers would start arguing and screaming at each other in Yiddish—just like in Galicia!

November turned into December, and soon a blanket of snow covered the prairie. Chanukah was coming, and the Jewish community of Grand Forks was in a flurry of activity.

There were *chanukiyot* to polish, dreidels to carve, Chanukah gelt to gather, candles to make, songs and blessings to rehearse.

And, of course, latkes to prepare.

On a cold, crisp December night, the Jews of Grand Forks, young and old, oldtimer and newcomer, gathered with their *chanukiyot*, their dreidels, their gelt, their small, simply wrapped gifts and filled the length and breadth of B'nai Israel's social hall. The room was filled with the smell of latkes frying in oil.

Together with the rabbi, they recited the blessings. *"Baruch atah Adonai Eloheinu Melech haolam, asher kid'shanu b'mitzvotav v'tzivanu l'hadlik ner shel Chanukah.*

Blessed are You, Eternal our God, Sovereign of the universe, who has made us holy by Your commandments and has commanded us to light the Chanukah candles."

Miriam chanted the next blessing with a clear voice that amazed even her parents: "*Baruch atah Adonai, Eloheinu Melech haolam, she-asah nisim laavoteinu bayamim haheim bazman hazeh.* Blessed are You, Eternal our God, Sovereign of the universe, who has performed miracles for our ancestors in times past and in our time."

Daniel led the Zalcman family in the final blessing: "*Baruch atah Adonai, Eloheinu Melech haolam, shehecheyanu, v'kiy'-manu v'higianu lazman hazeh.* Blessed are You, Eternal our God, who has kept us alive, who has sustained us and has brought us to this season."

With the lights of dozens of *chanukiyot* reflecting in the glass and dancing forth onto the prairie, the entire community replied, *"Amen v'amen."* Parents drew their children close and hugged them tightly. *"Chag samei-ach, gut yontiv,* a happy Chanukah!" Just like in Galicia.

Glossary

chanukiyah (plural: *chanukiyot*): The eight-branched Chanukah lamp. Its purpose is to remind us of the miracle of the lamp in the ancient Temple in Jerusalem that burned for eight days after the Syrians were defeated and the Temple was rededicated in 165 B.C.E.

dreidel: Yiddish for the four-sided top that children spin during the eight-day festival of Chanukah. The four Hebrew letters on each of its sides—*nun, gimel, hei, and shin*—stand for the Hebrew sentence *Nes gadol hayah sham*, "A great miracle happened there."

Galicia: Originally part of Poland, the province of Galicia was part of the Austro-Hungarian Empire from 1795 to 1918. During that period, Jews in Galicia enjoyed increased freedom and opportunity, particularly under Emperor Franz Josef II (1830–1916). From 1918 to 1939, all of Galicia was once again part of Poland. In 1939, Eastern Galicia became part of the Soviet Union and remained so until the collapse of the Soviet Union in 1991. Today, Western Galicia, including the city of Cracow, remains in Poland, while Eastern Galicia, including the city of Lvov, is part of the Ukraine.

gelt: Money or chocolates shaped as coins that are either given as presents to children or won during games of dreidel during the eight days of Chanukah.

Reb: The Yiddish equivalent of "Mr." or "Sir," and always a sign of honor and respect.

Shalom aleichem: "Peace unto you" in both Hebrew and Yiddish. It is the standard expression of fellowship among Jews and is responded to with the words *Aleichem shalom*, "Unto you, peace."

Tateh: The Yiddish word for "father." In Yiddish, one's father and mother are often combined into one word, *Tateh-Mameh*, meaning "parents."